Sending
Love, Empathy & Hope
♡ SissyMarySue

Dec. 6, 2021

Jelly Beans the Cheetah and Hope

Illustrated by Jacob Peterson
and Perpich Center Students

**Help Save the
Endangered
Cheetah!**

By SissyMarySue

(With a rhyming story for you!)

ISBN 13: 978-1-59298-911-9

Library of Congress Catalog Number: 2014917011

Printed in the United States of America

Fifth Printing: 2019

23 22 21 20 19   9 8 7 6 5

Beaver's Pond Press
7108 Ohms Lane
Edina, MN 55439–2129
952-829-8818

To order, visit www.sissymarysue.org
SissyMarySue is available for bookstore signings, classroom visits, teacher trainings, and speaking engagements.

SissyMarySue has partnered with two very important global organizations, H2o for Life and the Cheetah Conservation Fund.

H2o for Life educates, engages, and inspires youth to learn about the water crisis, take action, and become global citizens. To find out more about their organization and how you can help, please visit www.h2oforlifeschools.org.

The Cheetah Conservation Fund is the world's leading organization dedicated to saving the cheetah in the wild. To find out more about their organization and what you can do to help the cheetah in the race against extinction, please visit www.cheetah.org.

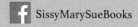 SissyMarySueBooks    @SissyMarySue   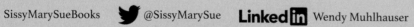 Wendy Muhlhauser   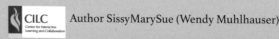 Author SissyMarySue (Wendy Muhlhauser)

Jelly Beans the Cheetah and Hope

Written by
SissyMarySue

Illustrations by
Jacob Peterson and
Perpich Center Students

To my son, Connor, my heart.

To the Barabaig Tribe, the inspiration for this book, who opened my eyes to the scarcity of basic needs in the world and taught me the beauty "to simply be."

To my dear mentors and friends — Hanna Kjeldbjerg, Sandy Schley, Karen Monson, Lee Truer, Nichole Smaglick, and Theresa Crawford—without whom this book would not exist.

To the twelve interns who embraced empathy and embodied compassionate action with their illustrations and support.

To my students, past and present, and all the youth of our world. This book is uniquely yours, and you are my ultimate inspiration.

To my mom, dad, my Ellison family, and all my dear friends for the love and support.

To the beautiful, but endangered, cheetah!

To others with brain injury—may this book give you hope to persevere!

And finally, I use this book to honor the brother-sister bond that I valued so greatly with my brother Dwayne (1962-1982). The memories of our connection resonate like a beautiful song.

There was a cheetah who grew up lonely and sad. His loving mother was all that he had. When she was taken away, he felt great sadness and dismay. He had grown up being teased, you see, for his spots looked different than they were supposed to be. They were oddly shaped instead of like dots. He was ridiculed, by others taking potshots. He felt like a freak, like he didn't belong. When his mother was there, she'd sing him a song. Her voice and the words of the song were so sweet. Knowing she loved him made him feel more complete.

"I love you, precious, sweet boy. You are my pride and joy. There is only one like you. Love yourself, as I love you, too. You have much to give—don't forget to love everyone as you live. Life is a gift for you to behold—don't forget to enjoy as you watch it unfold!" She always told him how precious he was, saying, "Your uniqueness is a gift, just because!" She explained, "Someday you'll learn why—it will give you joy, instead of making you cry." He learned how to love from his mother. She was a cheetah mother like no other.

The day he was captured he'll never forget. The other cheetahs laughed at him caught in the net. The men used a net since they wanted him alive. His unique markings gave them the idea to let him survive. He was afraid, and more alone than ever. The men talked about the cheetah, but didn't sound too clever. They had elaborate ideas to sell him. His life was looking increasingly dim.

When they finally got back to their base camp, they put him in a cage that felt cold and damp. One of the men had a daughter who lived with him there. She was beautiful, but sad, and had brown curly hair. Her name was Nichole, he would come to find out. By now the comforting words from his mother he was starting to doubt. His uniqueness got him into this situation. How could his uniqueness be good, was his contemplation. He was clearly losing hope. It was his mother's song that helped him cope. He believed, somehow, that she was right. The words of the song helped him hold on that first night.

The cheetah remained in the cage morning to night. This was just awful for him, far from delight. Nichole knew the endangered cheetah would die when confined. She was determined to help him by being kind. Nichole noticed the cheetah's sadness, too, just as he had noticed that she was blue. She could tell he was hurting about more because she had more empathy than before. They both cared deeply about each other. They were becoming like sister and brother.

Nichole learned cheetahs don't actually roar. She found his soothing purr hard to ignore. Nichole loved it when the cheetah purred. Somehow it made her feel reassured. Perhaps it's because while he purred, his mother's song played in his head. He kept her memory alive with her song and words that she'd said. The cheetah changed the song by replacing "boy" with "girl." He added a part about how Nichole's hair was all a-twirl. "I love you, precious, sweet girl. You have the most beautiful hair all a-twirl. There is only one like you. Love yourself, as I love you, too. You have much to give—don't forget to love everyone as you live. Life is a gift for you to behold— don't forget to enjoy as you watch it unfold!"

The cheetah felt good when he made Nichole happy for a while. He found that if he danced, that would make her smile. He would also rub up against the cage. Nichole was confident, regardless of her age. On top of the bars, she'd pet him as best she could. She didn't even question whether she should. They needed each other, like a sister and brother. Nichole gave the cheetah a name one day. "Your spots look like jelly beans, I have to say!"

Nichole didn't think he could understand or relate to what she said, but she still explained about her mother's song she sang in bed. While her mother was in hospice at home, Nichole would sit and stroke her hair with a comb. Her mother would quietly sing a "Jelly Beans" song. Nichole would help by loudly singing along. Her mom had given Nichole "Jelly Beans" as a nickname. It had profound meaning, but Nichole shared it just the same. The cheetah loved Jelly Beans as his new name. He was feeling loved without being the same. He was loved for his uniqueness, after all. This was a momentous occasion, not small.

Nichole sang the "Jelly Beans" song, without changing it or anyone singing along. "I love you, sweet Jelly Beans, my dear. You are bright, bold, and unique, that's clear. Dear Jelly Beans, you're here to fill the world with hope. With your loving, kind spirit you'll help others cope. Just as you've helped me, you will help countless others—you will see!" Nichole took a bow, declaring, "It's your song now!" They both had lost a mother, the real reason they needed each other.

One day Nichole's dad didn't come back. Nichole and Jelly Beans were all alone outside the empty shack. One day turned to twenty-three, so they wondered how their life would be. It was now a long time that her dad was away. Their food was low, and they wondered where they should stay.

All this time Jelly Beans had been learning to talk. He uttered Nichole's name as she headed out for a walk. Jelly Beans was worried she would get hurt. Nichole was amazed by him delivering that blurt! "Wow, you actually said my name!" Jelly Beans replied, "I can say more words just the same!"

Nichole went on to more completely explain, "I was headed to the tribe across the plain. I met a village elder named Mbee-sha* there. He seemed so loving, I think he would care. Maybe he would help me and you. Although, I don't know if they'd let you live there, too."

*Em-bee-sha

Then Nichole knelt by Jelly Beans and said, "I should let you go free, since a cage is no place for a beautiful animal to be." He'd never been called beautiful before except by his mother, whom he surely did adore. "I don't care if I'm in trouble if my dad ever comes back. It was wrong of him to put you in a cage by our shack! I love you, Jelly Beans, my dear, but it is wrong to keep you here. You belong in the wild, to be free like a child."

Jelly Beans asked, "Are you sure?" Nichole said lovingly, "Jelly Beans, you are so pure! Yes I'm sure, you have given me hope. I feel like now I'm more able to cope. Your love for me was an absolute gift. It helped me make a miraculous shift. I love you so much that I want you to be free. I want what's best for you, you see!"

With that, Nichole unlocked the cage door. The two hugged as they never could before. Tears streamed down each of their cheeks. It felt like they'd been together longer than a mere six weeks. "Go run to your freedom, dearest one," Nichole encouraged after their long hug was done. Jelly Beans bolted and ran away very fast. He ran seventy miles an hour again, at last!

It felt so good to be free, but he wondered about Nichole, so turned around to see. He could tell she was crying, but happy with what she'd done. Then Jelly Beans changed his mind and the direction of his run. He turned completely around, which was something quite profound. Nichole was surprised and quite amazed. Jelly Beans was exhausted and a little dazed.

Nichole asked, "What in the world are you doing back here? Why didn't you keep running, Jelly Beans, my dear?" Jelly Beans explained, "Your unselfishness in setting me free inspired me to re-think where I wanted to be. It's my deepest desire to make sure that you thrive. I hunt during the day, which could help keep you alive. I can protect you while you're asleep at night. I can be there during the day, in plain sight."

Jelly Beans and Nichole walked to the village side by side. Now that they decided to stay together, they hoped they could live with the tribe. Mbeesha* smiled broadly when he saw Nichole and Jelly Beans coming near. "I was worried you two were alone, I'm glad that you came here." Nichole gushed, "Mbeesha,* you are so kind! Jelly Beans and I can stay here, you wouldn't mind?" The Barabaig** family welcomed the two, showing beautiful empathy, as they do.

*Em-bee-sha **Bar-a-bag

Feeling a greater connection to the human family, they felt settled and embraced their gift to simply be. Jelly Beans was inspired to share how Nichole had helped him cope. To honor her, he wanted to give her the name of Hope. He told her she had absolutely given him that, since he had felt so alone in the cage where he sat. "You helped me feel less alone in that horrible cage. Because of you I felt hope, even in that dark stage." They had now both done the same by giving each other a special new name.

The Barabaig* tribe needed clean water close by, so humanitarians made them an earth dam the color of sky. One night when Jelly Beans and Hope had been asleep for a while, a child snuck into their mud hut with a mischievous smile. The humanitarians had brought markers that were bold and bright. One child used them to fill in Jelly Beans markings that night. In the morning, Jelly Beans and Hope laughed loud and strong. They both figured it was what needed to happen all along.

*Bar-a-bag

Jelly Beans now fully embodied his name. With those markings, it's good he was tame. Hope spoke quietly, tilting her head to the side, while taking in Jelly Beans' confidence and pride. "You've persevered and found your self-esteem, and all because of the Barabaig* tribe, it would seem!"

*Bar-a-bag

Everyone loved his colorful, Jelly Beans fur. He expressed his gratitude through his soothing purr. It was all making beautiful sense now. His mother's words enlightened him, wow! She'd been right about it all. Everyone has a unique call. He finally understood how our connection to all makes it impossible to feel insignificant or small. Connection provides us with a sense of our wholeness. It empowers us with empathy, true confidence, and boldness. Jelly Beans realized it was their mothers who had taught the two that giving love is the most meaningful and powerful thing to do.

THE BARABAIG TRIBE

The Barabaig tribe has much to teach us about the beauty of knowing how to simply be. They are an emotionally available, loving, and grateful people living in a village in Tanzania, Africa. They are very openly affectionate, and have a spiritual leader and village elders as their structure of governance. I went to Tanzania with the Edina Rotary Club in 2007 to view an earth dam that had been built through our club in partnership with a club in Dar es Salaam. We stayed with the tribe and interacted with many individuals. One of the village elders named Mbeesha had a particularly luminous spirit, and I am grateful for the opportunity to honor him in this story.

<u>Housing:</u> Members of the Barabaig tribe live in mud huts. When constructing the huts, the division of labor is set with the men building the structure and the women applying the mud. When it rains, the women repair these structures by adding additional mud.

<u>Lifestyle:</u> The Barabaig are a nomadic tribe, and rely on cattle herding as a source of milk, meat, and leather. Cattle are treated as currency, and are very valuable. They are polygamists, having more than one wife.

<u>Clothing:</u> The simple manner in which the Barabaig wear their cloth is significant in distinguishing between the Barabaig and the Maasai tribe (another Tanzanian nomadic tribe). The Maasai tie their cloth near a shoulder, while the Barabaig simply drape their cloth. Barabaig men wear mostly red colors like the Maasai, but also wear blue, green, and other colors. Men, women, and children wear black sandals made of recycled tires. The young women wear beautiful, beaded, brown leather dresses; each dress is handmade and takes approximately three months to create. The dresses are worn always, except during childbirth. The older women wear brown, fringed leather dresses that are less extravagant looking. Women, and some men, wear multiple bracelets. It was absolutely imperative for me to accurately depict the cultural specifics of the tribe as a way to honor them. That was why I chose to lead and monitor every aspect of the illustration process in order to make sure that happened.

<u>Significance of the Earth Dam:</u> Unlike tribes where women carry things on their heads, women in the Barabaig tribe carry water in a gourd placed in a basket that they carry like a backpack. Before the earth dam was built near the village, it was the job of the young girls to get water. They were sent out at night (when it was cool) to walk miles and miles to where the water source was. This is when the predators were out, too! Many girls could not go to school due to this. To witness, up close, their deep gratitude for simply being alive—even without basic needs met—was humbling and life changing to me. To see the lives of the tribe significantly improve due to this earth dam was profound. The harmony and peacefulness I felt among the Barabaig tribe and how they embraced all mankind, including our group of foreign humanitarians, reached me in the depth of my being. It provided me with a connection to mankind and to all. It empowered me with more empathy and to be a voice for what I had experienced. I was compelled to teach about the scarcity of basic needs for most in the world and about the beauty of the tribe. I did that for four years, which is what led me to write a book that ignites the imaginations of young people, encouraging them to care about the needs in our world, to see the beauty of the tribe I had the privilege and honor to stay with, and about the beauty of Africa. One custom of the Barabaig tribe is to give each other meaningful names, so I was deeply honored when I was given the name "Udenda,"which means "likes to fetch water and feed her family." I hope that this book helps honor the caretaker and teacher characteristics they saw in me—I will always take care of my human family!

CRITICAL THINKING QUESTIONS

This book has been implemented in classrooms ranging from preschool to middle school. Modify the questions and the rate at which you read the book to fit the needs of your class (the entire book does not need to be read in one day).

1. What are some of the words that you are not familiar with? Are there clues you can find on the pages to help you figure out their meaning? (There is a complete vocabulary word list with their definitions at www.sissymarysue.com if you get stumped, but I know that you can figure them out!)

2. Nichole feels "empathy" for Jelly Beans when he is in the cage. Do you know what empathy means? Who else shows empathy in the story? In what ways do they show it?

3. How and why does the Barabaig tribe show empathy to Nichole and Jelly Beans?

4. Why were Jelly Beans and Nichole both sad? How did they help each other?

5. What did the main characters find that they had in common? What did they give to each other that was similar?

6. The Barabaig have many specific details about their culture. What are the culturally specific details you see in the illustrations? What do they wear as clothing? What do their houses look like? They also share things in common with us. How are they the same as we are?

7. Do you know what is meant by "human family" or "shared humanity"? If everyone in the world does not have basic needs like clean water, what can we do to help? Why should we help?

8. Why did the humanitarians build the Barabaig tribe an earth dam? What do you think an earth dam is? (Hint: It collects rain water.) What else did they give to the children?

9. Did you know the cheetah is endangered? Do you know what that means? There are many cheetah facts in the story. What are they? Learn more about the cheetah and Dr. Laurie Marker's work to save the cheetah from extinction at Cheetah Conservation Fund: www.cheetah.org.

10. At the end of the story, Jelly Beans embraces his uniqueness, finding his wholeness. What makes him unique? What makes him finally feel whole? Who helped him find his self-esteem? Who else is unique in the story?

11. Both Jelly Beans' and Nichole's mothers embraced their uniqueness. What is special about you that makes you unique?

12. What do we share in common with all people? What do we share in common with all living beings on Earth?

13. What did Jelly Beans' mother teach him?

14. What did Jelly Beans and Nichole's mothers teach them that is "the most meaningful and powerful thing to do"?

Ideas for Interactive Learning (Drama/Play for Learning)

Pre-K – 1st Grade: I recommend reading just a few pages a day to the younger students, combining this with interactive activities like constructing a simple mud hut, cage, the earth dam (a circle of chairs works great), and other items from the story. Using drama/play for learning will bring the messages from the book to life. Re-create some or all of the scenes from the book together. Have fun playing! Once familiar with the story, educators can reinforce vocabulary skills and language learning by stopping just short of the rhyme and letting the children fill in the words. Another suggestion is to utilize this book for foreign language education, especially for color vocabulary and counting Jelly Beans' markings.

2nd Grade – 6th Grade: Recreating scenes from the book works well for older students, as well. The making of an elaborate mud hut is a great activity for older students because it helps reinforce the Barabaig tribe's division of labor, with the men building the structure and the women applying the mud. I use a large piece of brown fabric for the mud and long sticks to build the structure (with the help of tape and a circle of chairs). The construction of the hut facilitates spatial thinking, problem solving, and teamwork. Students discover how to create peace and harmony, which is essential to accomplish this since it is a student-only activity! It builds great confidence and emotional competence in the face of pressure and a new challenge.

Visit the website for additional support, more information about drama/play for learning, and for an audio recording of the book and its songs. www.sissymarysue.com

WALL OF EMPATHY

Thank you to the kind contributors who "empowered our youth with empathy to spring into compassionate action" with their generous donations towards the production cost of this book. Your support and encouragement meant more to me than you know. This book would not exist without the collective effort of us all.

Johnny and Whitney Ellison

Dr. Laurie Marker (honorary)

Brian and Barbara Hamill   Dr. Tony and Pastor Joy Grainger   Miss Katie

Paul Grainger (in memory)   Dr. Onaiza Ansar   Brett McSparron   Cathy Williams

Deepa Mathur   Maureen Muhlhauser   Byron and Kim Dorgan   Paul R. Mooty

Karen Muhlhauser   Dr. Paul and Ailene Muhlhauser   Dr. Sandy and Duane Schley   Dahje Holmes

Paul and Ruth Durand   Mary and Elise Breckman   Dwayne and E.J. Muhlhauser (in memory)

Harambee Elementary staff and students

Crosswinds Arts and Science School staff and students

25

ACKNOWLEDGMENTS

A book isn't created by one mind, heart, or person. It is an inspired and beautifully collaborative, collective effort! I believe we are absolutely the sum of our parts. There are so many to acknowledge for contributing to this book's creation. Thank you to all who have loved and believed in me, especially in relation to my publishing journey. Thank you to the countless people who influenced me in my formative years and beyond. I encourage you all to take personal ownership of this book with me. I could not have done it without the inspiration, influence, and support of every one of you!

Thank you to Beaver's Pond Press for believing in this book and me as a writer. Thank you to the Barabaig tribe and the clean water project by Edina Rotary—the inspiration for this book. Thank you to the luminous, welcoming village elder named Mbeesha, honored in this book. Thank you to Dad for inspiring me with your entrepreneurship and Rotary service. Thank you Rotary International for the work you do in our world to benefit people whose basic needs are not met, and thank you for the honor to be a part of that work.

I am grateful for the beautiful fellowship in Edina Rotary, especially for my friends Dr. Sandy Schley, Tim Murphy, Paul Mooty, Bob Perkins, San Asato, Dr. Ellen Kennedy, Dr. Arthur Rouner, Jennifer Bennerotte, Audri Schwarz, Greg Hanks, Joel Jennings, Bill McReavy Jr. (who cares deeply about loss), and Bob Solheim (a man who fully encapsulates empathy and love as director of N.C. Little Hospice).

Thanks to my entire Ellison family, especially Johnny, Whitney, and Tristan for your love, stability, and support throughout my life and particularly on this journey.

Thank you to the Grainger family, whose son I loved in college. I am honored to have had your love and support as a constant in my life beyond your son's death.

Thank you for all who encouraged me to not go small with the vision I had for this book, including: Mom; Connor Willgohs (my son, the original "precious sweet boy"); Theresa Crawford; Uncle Brian and Aunt Barbara; Dahje Holmes; Ace Carter; Kemiah Cook; Phil Breckman; Cindy Awes; Gary Lehr; Mary Arnold; Rebecca Moir; Candy Quilling; Dr. David Lund; Cathy Williams; the wonderful Crosswinds and Harambee staff and students (especially Torria Randall, Ralonda Mckinley, Lorean Greene, Corneilus Rish, Brynda Sengbusch, Todd Weinhold, Peggy Palumbo, Kathy Griebel, Lindsay Most, Abeba Merkuria, Denise Dzik, Melissa and Doug Kleemeier, Larry Dunnigan, and Jessica Morgan); and my neighbors and friends (Missy Preiner, Tina Wollmuth, Nancy King, Keith Amborn, Annie Buck, Ann Benjamin, Al Kelpser, and Jim Ford). Thank you, too, my dear friends from my neighborhood printing shop, Joe, Rishi, and Nic. Thanks to the innovative designers Laura Drew and Justin Schwingle.

Thank you to my generous mentors for their friendship and support: thank you, Hanna Kjeldbjerg from Beaver's Pond Press, who delivered a uniquely magical and beautiful collaboration. This book found its full depth as a result of your support and influence. Thank you for empowering me as a writer through your brilliance, friendship, and thoughtfulness, and for illuminating every meeting with your genuine sparkle!

Thank you, Dr. Sandy Schley. Thank you for inviting me to Africa to see first-hand how our Edina Rotary Club helped the lives of the Barabaig people. This opened my eyes to the scarcity of basic needs for most in the world. I chose you as the face of humanitarianism in the end of the book because of your humility and unequaled humanitarian service. Your invitation to Tanzania, Africa, absolutely inspired the personal and professional growth that led to this book. Thank you for supporting me every step of the way on this literary journey.

Thank you, Karen Monson. Thank you for welcoming me to Perpich Center for Arts Education, for overseeing the illustration interns, and for empowering me in a completely new area as only you can do. You were an essential presence in my life, providing the encouraging words that kept me confident when I encountered obstacles with the book beyond the Perpich phase of development.

Thank you, Lee Truer, my graduate advisor at St. Mary's University in the Human Development Program. Lee, your belief in me and unique support provided me with the confidence I needed for my graduate work, for my literary pursuit, and for building SissyMarySue LLC.

Thank you, Nichole Smaglick. I used your image and name for the Nichole character in the book to honor your contribution in alerting the Edina Rotary to the Barabaig's needs. Thanks for introducing me to the full beauty of Africa—its people and the animals on safari—and for encouraging me to help with Cheetah Conservation.

There are twelve interns to thank for having provided the true beauty and strength of this literary pursuit. High-school age illustration interns: Jacob Peterson, Shelby Graves, and Kylie Yeigh. College-age marketing and business interns: Stacy Dahl, Ngoc Nguyen, Olivia Skyberg, Francelia Dennis, and Lily Jacobson (from St. Catherine's University in St.Paul); Katie Grout (from Inver Hills Community College); Dearris Judkins, David Jones, and Ethan "Mr. Music" Horace (from IPR-The Institute of Production and Recording College). To have you all take ownership of the messages of the book—and work so diligently to deliver them to the youth in our world by illustrating and supporting this book—is more than powerful. It is inspiring and comforting to witness the sincere depth and commitment to our world that you all so beautifully exemplify!

Thank you to Perpich Center for Arts Education, where I experienced creativity and critical thinking inextricably linked. Thank you, Sue Mackert, Dr. Carlondrea Hines, Duane Dutrelle, and Lynn Delisi for joining me to help bring this book to the world.

Thank you to the beautiful cheetah I saw on a safari in Africa who inspired the cheetah character. It is a distinct privilege to help save the endangered cheetah! Thank you, Dr. Laurie Marker for forming an alliance with SissyMarySue LLC and endorsing the book as a way to spread the message about saving the endangered cheetah. I am honored to support your tireless, wide-reaching work to save the cheetah from extinction through Cheetah Conservation Fund.

Thanks to other supportive colleagues in my beloved education field, especially superintendents Dr. Ric Dressen and Paul Durand. Thanks, too, to Lori Murphy, Denise Gustafson, Kayla Ganje, Darby Lent, Kerry Gautsch, Brittany Clausell, Willie Finley, Julian McFaul, Josh Fraser, Anthony Scott, Tammy Albers, Kathleen Mortenson, Jean Sorensen, and Joni Hagebock. Thanks for the support to teach from this book, especially at Harambee Elementary School, Edina Community Ed., Crosswinds Arts and Science School, and Intergenerational Learning Center (when it was still in the production process). Thanks, teachers and staff from Brooklyn Center High School, especially Kris Edmonds and Erin Drake who suggested Jacob Peterson as the illustrator.

Many other people influenced and supported me, including: my Ellison brothers John Jr. and Jamie Ellison; my dear friend Dr. Onaiza Ansar; my step-mom Karen Muhlhauser; Karen Read Dobrzynski; my brothers Paul (the originator of my pen name, SissyMarySue), Robert, Jacob, and Nick; my aunts, uncles, and cousins, especially Uncle Byron, Uncle Darrell, Aunt Kim, and Aunt Kathy; my gymnastics coach, Gil Salazar; Pastor Rick Halvorson, Pastor Laurie Natwick, Pastor Kathy Fick, and Pastor Robert Hall; my high school teachers Mr. Lowery (Philosophy), Mr. Jelle (Government), and my AP Grammar/Composition teacher Mrs. Wall, who taught me to make every word mean something.

I want to also share that I am grateful for every aspect of my life, both easy and difficult, since it provided me with strength and the introspective mind that led me to write. I truly believe that challenges are a tremendous gift if we choose to harness what can be learned from them. I believe that the heart that gave me the desire to write and share comes directly from all of that. I loved the opportunity to share the magic of rhyme for brain healing and brain development with others. It was a gift to get to share! It felt like a miracle, too, since I struggled for many years with reading and writing following brain injuries. Thanks for taking the time to read the acknowledgment pages! In that, you helped me honor all who have contributed to my being able to write and produce this book.

Thank you! Sending Great Appreciation and JOY, SissyMarySue.

SISSYMARYSUE is a lifelong Minnesota educator with an MA in Human Development. She is widely recognized for her innovative Jelly Beans Creative Learning approach that focuses on emotional competence, critical thinking, cultural sensitivity, language learning, and the natural world. After retiring the Jelly Beans Creative Learning brand she launched SissyMarySue, producing books that focus on literacy, emotional competence, critical thinking, and world themes. Using her books as content, her play/drama approach has been effectively implemented in many classrooms from pre-K to middle school, including for foreign language learning through its incorporation in Spanish language curriculum.

Through speaking and training, SissyMarySue demonstrates her philosophy that empowering youth with empathy and an understanding of our shared humanity results in more tolerance, peacefulness, and harmony. Classroom management is less of an issue when we empower our youth with empathy, equipping them with emotional competence. This kind of empowerment has great potential to inspire youth to spring into compassionate action in their communities and in service for their world.

In this unique collaboration, the illustrators were all high school students when they began! The first two student illustrators attended Perpich Center for Arts Education. SHELBY GRAVES masterfully created the Jelly Beans the Cheetah character with whimsy and accuracy, as well as the other cheetah characters. KYLIE YEIGH is responsible for most of the people, capturing important details to represent the actual people they were based upon. She encapsulated expressions in the most exquisite way so we can feel what the character feels. Kylie's work expanded beyond people and she continued her work beyond high school, creating the amazing cover based on the first image ever created for the story by Shelby.

JACOB PETERSON, a student from Brooklyn Center High School, worked to polish the book and create a uniform aesthetic, modifying every page to provide even more cultural specifics to honor and accurately depict the Barabaig tribe. Jacob was dedicated and advanced the book to the finish line, which is how he earned his name on the cover. Jacob also created original images, and conceived the idea of demonstrating humanitarianism with the oval depicting the earth dam and the humanitarian giving markers to the child. He designed the precious and powerful silhouette used on the last page of the book, as well.

Each artist is of equal importance to the book, artistically. In fact, the cover has contributions from all three illustrators which is quite remarkable, since it is seamless. The beauty of this collaboration is due to the combination of these creative minds working to interpret the text, sharing their ideas, talents, time, and hearts to bring this story to stunning visual life.